This igloo book belongs to:

....

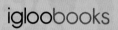

Published in 2016
by Igloo Books Ltd
Cottage Farm
NN6 0BJ
www.igloobooks.com

LEO002 0616
2 4 6 8 10 9 7 5 3 1
ISBN 978-1-78557-735-2

Printed and manufactured in China

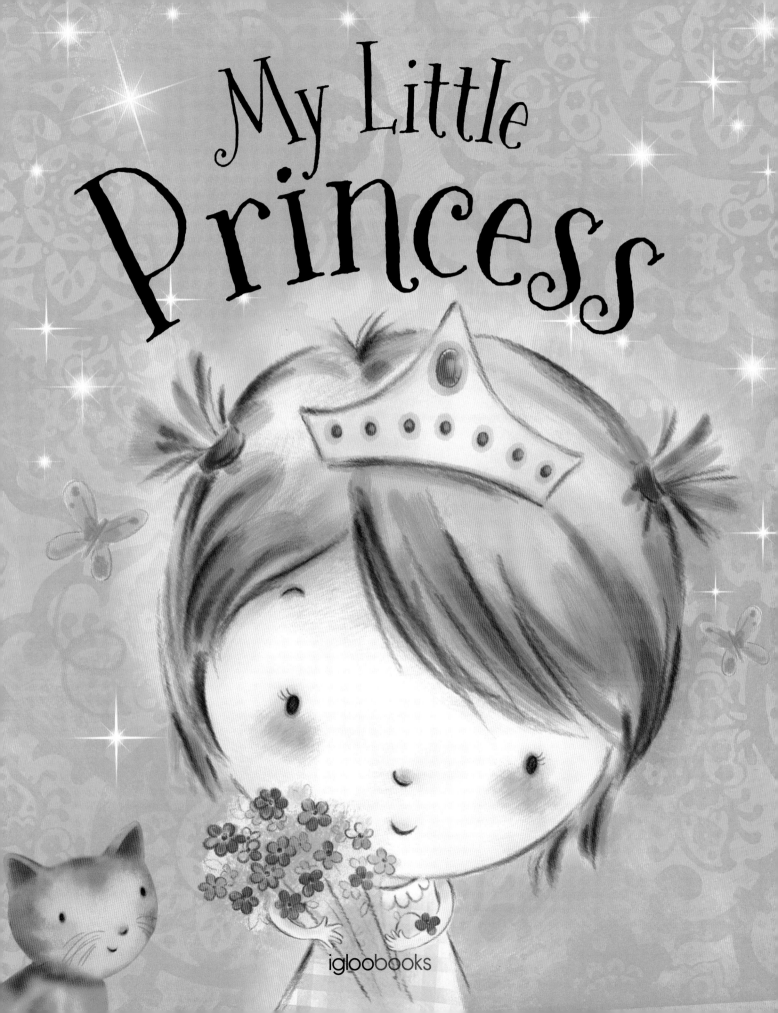

My Little
Princess

igloobooks

A real princess doesn't need
a castle or a throne.
Her natural charm and smarts
create a style all her own.

Dressed up in royal-blue jeans
and some shades for extra flair,
she cartwheels through the kingdom
as the sunshine combs her hair!

Her happily-ever-laughter
fills the air just like a song.
She makes the world a sweeter place,
she does it all day long!

Her mirror isn't magic,
but it's always impressed.
Believing in herself is what
a princess does the BEST!

She crowns each day with kindness,
spreading joy throughout the land.
Whenever she's around, a
friend is always close to hand!

There's no doubt about it,
she's the brightest star in the sky.
She sparkles like a diamond
and she doesn't even try.

Stick a photo of your
princess here.

My Little Princess

A princess is a wish come true.
Believe me, I should know!
I've got one of my very own,
I'll never let you go!

A real princess doesn't need
a castle or a throne.
Her natural charm and smarts
create a style all her own.